I0748563

FARZANEHGY

FARZANEHGY

Mohsen Hariri

Daniel Hariri

Mohsen Hariri

Contents

FARZANEHGY

PREFACE

Preface

This book is dedicated to my Son Daniel.

This book is an attempt to depict the East for the Western society in a novel with Ali as its main character. Ali is born in the East and he is an immigrant living in the West. He immigrated to the West a long time ago. Our story is about his life in the East as a child, his experiences growing up in the East, the difficulties for him to get settled in the West, his difficulties as a grown up now living in the West but above all his personal evolution which resulted for him to try to be the most useful member of the society wherever he would choose to live.

Today we have such mix of societies in the West as never before and that has caused two issues.

Firstly, Eastern people coming to west sometimes forget their origins and fail to learn what best the West has to offer. Needless to say, all science, technology and medicine progress today is all done in the West so there is no doubt of the successfully operating society of the West.

Secondly, the Eastern reality of life is mostly hidden also even for the majority of the native people. Habits and behaviours are mandated by an unknown legacy with a generation to generation progress of what is, or what is not acceptable. Today, these original traditions are nearly failing even in the East, not only because of the extreme rapid changes of contemporary way of life, but also due to the misinterpretation of the Eastern culture concepts. This misinterpretation of the wealthy Eastern culture has caused most unreasonable behaviour and the formation of some wicked governing bodies now operating in the East. Hopefully this book may be able to enlighten some facts that in turn could clarify how some evil acts are ridiculously justified in the East.

Not only the first or even the second generation of the immigrants, but also the new immigrants coming to West, face numerous dilemma of right or wrong. The question of what to do and how to proceed with one's life extends even to the western people who happen to engage in family relationships with the eastern people. Such relationships require convergence of not only personal principle, taste and habits, but also requirements that extend to dealing with issues such as differences in people's religion, race or even how the immediate family members would react to the individual's chosen relationship.

Utmost attempt is made to avoid restricting the concept of this book to a person living in a specific country, religion, race or sexual orientation and any deviation from this is unintentional. Any names mentioned in this book are fictional and resemblance to any real person is accidental. Special thanks to my Son Daniel who has contributed to the writing of this book by being my own mirror, Daniel has helped me by listening to my thoughts and commenting on them. Daniel has also done beautiful illustrations for this book.

Mohsen Hariri
06/02/2022

1

CHAPTER ONE

Chapter One

Ali is born in the East, Ali's Childhood

Ieki boud, ieki naboud, gheir az Khoda hich kas naboud.

This is the usual way of beginning to tell a story in the East and basically means Once upon a time

One stormy night, in a small house and in a country in the East was born a boy named Ali. His father had a very good job and his mother was a housewife as was quite customary for women not to work in those days. In his family there was one first born boy, then three girls and then himself, he was the smallest in the family and hence grew up to be a very cared after, always well dressed chubby toddler. He had long, dark brown hair, black eyes and a lot of toys and clothing, much more than any other boy in their greater family of cousins, his nephew or even in their neighbourhood. He always wished to grow up very quickly and go to school like his bigger sisters because they seemed to be having a lot of fun. However he was not getting any attention early in the mornings when his dad was leaving home and his Mother was preparing his sisters to go to school. He always wished to explore the world outside his home, he wished to meet his future to be classmates in the neighbourhood but there were no playgrounds or parks near where he lived. He was thinking that when he grew up to school age, even just walking together with his classmates to school every day would be quite an adventure.

Ali remembers as a child to be living in a busy family, his first born bigger brother had a wife and family of his own. Not only Ali's family was big but he had also loads of cousins, a nephew and a niece. His niece and most cousins were nearly his own age because his parents had great age differences with their brothers and sisters and so their children were about his own age and so was his age difference with his brother. Ali enjoyed playing with all of them on frequent visits which was customary at the time between families. However his best memories were of the time when everyone was gathering at his grandparent's house where all children would be there and could play with little surveillance from the grown-ups. Even as a child he was surprised to notice that bigger children were separated as boys and girls from a certain age. Girls would usually spend most of their time in the kitchen together with their Mums and grandmother. They would all help in cooking, while drinking tea and gossiping; whereas boys would play outside, watch or listen to the news in TV or radio and listen to their Dads and grandfather discussing business and the latest news or any current family matter.

Even from small age Ali was taught that as a boy he had to be hard and strong, he should never cry and that he had the responsibility of helping and defending every other family member but most important his Mother and his sisters. It was then that he was being familiarised with the notion of considering his Mother and his sisters as his Namous and the act of defending them as his Gheirat.

Ali learnt that having Gheirat and protecting his Namous was considered of crucial importance. Unfortunately that was especially true for the grown ups and things could turn nasty because of it. It was not unknown for things to go real nasty and even in the first relation relatives, in order to keep the family values. Real heart breaking actions were not unheard of, such as declaring your own son or daughter as an Apostate for whom the family would not care any more and their names let forgotten. Any action of approaching the Apostate or sometimes even the mention of their name was considered taboo. The Apostate's name would soon be forgotten by everyone except for the very old women in every family who would somehow magically know everything and remember everything that had ever happened in the family and as far as in their neighbourhood and even in their far fetched families. Apostates, as such, were very young boys or girls and usually even in their teens, which were guilty of only simple natural mistakes because of their prohibited behaviour. These youth's only mistake was a daring to take things slightly further than what would have been possibly acceptable by the society which was a touch or a kiss. Apostates would usually move to big cities where they could have a new beginning of their lives and on their own.

In the East, schools were separate for girls and boys from their childhood and it seemed that everything was designed to be in line with a pre marriage hermit life. Even as a child, Ali was wondering if this separation should really begin so early in life, rather than later during the secondary school years. There was no reason for why he should be separated from his sister who was only one year older than himself for if they were going to the same school, they could have spent more time together. Ali wished for the day when first attending primary schools boys and girls would be allowed together, just to play with each other and to get to know each other better. Likewise, he thought it was quite ridiculous to require a small girl to wear any kind of Hejab, surely it was only to accustom a young mind into wearing a head covering but it is simply ridiculous and ruining their childhood.

Girls' high schools were always crowded outside; Ali remembered seeing older mischievous boys gathering around or near girls' schools. The boys would usually just sit around in groups and hang around waiting until the time when girl's school would be closing. Then they would shout comments about girls dress or the way they walked. Girls would also be in groups and would just shy or giggle away from the boys. Ali couldn't help but thinking of the possibility that these innocent children could be the future Apostates of their own neighbourhood.

His Mum was always telling him that one day he will grow up to marry a girl of good heart and from a good family. The word "girl" would be particularly emphasised so as to distinguish between girls that were previously married and hence were referred to as women or ladies. A woman or a lady would suit a more mature man and that a young man should always seek girls' acquaintances and wisely choose between them.

Even as a child Ali found it strange how separated most families were in respect to the husband and wife relationship. There seemed to be a certain chasm in husband and wife's connection, where the understanding of simple characteristic differences was missing. Of course the husband would not be aware of the sometimes moody character of his wife and her expectations of an ideal husband. For so many years he has been only dealing with other men or boys and it is only now that he has got the opportunity of marriage and he is bound to spend most of his time with his other half. By encountering such different behaviour from his woman to what the man has been used to all his life, he grows rather cold. The husband is usually unaware of his wife's depth of love and devotion to him and decides to indulge more in his career rather than to try in order to better understand his wife. The decision to give himself up to his job results in him spending less time with his wife and usually make the differences more, despite possibly sweeter time spent while together. Ali believed that husbands usually simply don't know how to best approach their wives and that the sudden change of their hermit life to a family life is too much for them to cope with. Ali considered this change to be equally challenging for both the man and the woman in the relationship, he also thought that the challenge to be harder, the older the marriage age for both men and women.

Most women knew little of what their husbands did during all the long hours of work when they were gone, all they knew was their husband is for example a carpenter, a baker or a chef and that they were out doing their job. Any details of their job, whom they met during their business or any kind of their specific job difficulties, were unknown to the wives. Likewise, men also knew nothing of their wives problems; all they knew was that their wives were at home cooking and raising children. All Men knew from their children's growth, was when and which one needed a new shoe or clothing so that they would know how much extra money they should add to the usual weekly or monthly household allowance.

The family's savings, future planning and even public relations were mostly one-sidedly decided by the man. If they were changing their home, even the decorations inside the house, what kitchen appliances to get was the men's decision. Even when the children would grow older, it was the man's decision who their daughters would marry. Ali himself knew numerous examples of this accustomed behaviour of the family man, although Ali's own family was more liberal.

It was hence assumed that all the responsibility for the children's raising and nurture was done by women and men only had to provide their financial support. Despite women's such great responsibility, their great effort for their household and their success in life was mostly hidden and confined to their house. The success of a great housewife was only apparent when you visited their home and witnessed the cleanliness, tidiness and order in their house and the look of their children and their success in school.

Unfortunately men did little to help women at home and it was not unknown that men would even behave badly for things going wrong at home, instead of giving a helping hand. It was not unheard of, for example that a man would throw away forcefully and break a salt shaker because it happened to have no salt in it. Of course it would be unimaginable for the husband to get up and fill it up with salt himself because that was a woman's job. Another usual example was for men to throw away food that wasn't cooked properly right outside the window. Ali knew of such examples listening to his Mum's friends and acquaintances either while they had gone shopping or for a visit to their neighbours or a friend's house. Such matters, even if they existed, would be rarely discussed during family gatherings to avoid embarrassments and so such issues were never really resolved. The only solution seemed to be for the woman to be more alert and careful of all the details and aspects of her household to avoid disappointment.

On the other hand women also sometimes pointed out the excessive success of their neighbour or a family compared to their own, to their husbands. The housewife would mention that their neighbours for example could afford specific gadgets or cars but they couldn't. Then the occasional quarrel between husbands and wives was quite usual which would usually end only as "we need to stop the quarrel because of the children" and not because they would reach to any specific result or resolution in order to improve their life and success.

It was not as if there was any specific problem or quarrel going on that would upset the family but just a constant unease between the husband and wife possibly due to their formal relationship, that is, the man and woman were husband and wife before they could be friends. Even as a child Ali could see this formality nearly everywhere and more or less in every family. He felt that this needed to change, that is to say, if there was more love and understanding in the family, most issues were resolved. It was not as if his parents did not love him or one another, he could see their affection for each other in their eyes and a very rare, that special touch of the hands. However, it was as if the expression of affection was forbidden. If they were alone and only with their children present, a light touch of each others hands or a sweet glimpse of each other with a smile would be considered as acceptable. There seemed to be some belief, some unspoken arrangement that was keeping them apart in a dreadful formality, some kind of a prototype or a simple shyness that prevented nearly every man to show his affection to his wife even in front of their own children.

Ali thought this should be something that men have to do and possibly what he himself will need to do when he grew up, that is, men should not show any affection. Ali's father would never even hug him or kiss him dearly as he would usually do only for his birthdays or when once Ali fell seriously ill. Ali could never imagine himself as the male prototype he knew and was learning about. He wanted to change things when he grew up, to share and embrace all work and responsibilities with his future partner in life and to openly show his love and affection to his wife and children. Even as a child, Ali knew that this change would not be easy but he was unsure how even he himself would turn out to be as a father and when he grew up to have a family of his own.

There were also families of relatives whose father had gone out to the West to study and had returned to marry a girl in their own traditional way. Those families were mostly having a better structure and a seemingly better husband and wife relationship. Ali was wondering if this improvement was due to their education, which made the difference for the better or it was simply the fact that the Graduates from the West have had certain social experiences that had deeply affected and improved them. One thing was for sure that they mostly tended to have fewer children in their family. They had mostly only one, two or rarely at most three children and hence each child could get better attention. Also the husband and wife relationship seemed to be more loving, settled and stable, though having the same general structure. Ali didn't know of any family whose mother would have gone abroad, possibly because it was considered bad for girls to stay away from their family before marriage and when married, they would get stuck to their household.

Ali sincerely believed a change was definitely necessary, however, it was not everything that Ali considered in need of changing and he found that he fully respected certain formalities in the society. For example when men at the market, bazaar, were caught swearing to each other by his Mum, they nearly even blushed and were apologetic and had uneasy behaviour when they found out that what they said was overheard by a woman. Also, marriage was considered truly sacred and an important event which was involved a huge preparation from both families of husband and wife. The share of each family as to the contribution to the marriage ceremony and all that was needed for marriage life was also outlined by the tradition although could differ from place to place. The marriage celebration sometimes lasted even for days in far away villages.

Another example of a good formality may be the notion of "Mehrieh" which could be translated as dowry. Mehrieh is the amount of money the groom promises as insurance for the bride to guarantee her future should the marriage be broken up. It is a deeply rooted fact and belief in the society that Mehrieh should never be given or taken by anyone. However Mehrieh should be considered but just as a provision to ensure for the future well being of the bride, especially when children are involved.

In short, Ali saw himself against an outdated, very deeply rooted public prototype which needed to be eased. The change in the prototype should still keep the deeply rooted mutual respect and the provision for women and children in the society while at the same time would be able to break the ice in husband and wife relationship. A simple change in the prototype as a possible solution for example could be having mixed primary schools as a first step. Such simple change ensures that at least children could experience a basic understanding of each other from early age while boys and girls could freely play with each other. A next step could be having all schools mixed as a pilot scheme with separate classes for boys and girls in the same school and according to regional requirements. Ali was sure that there should be more ways to improve the private daily life while keeping community values intact. He wished for the implementation of any changes that could bring about a more natural and free society with smooth, normalised family relationships.

It was in such conditions that Ali spent his childhood and such was his thoughts and feelings about it, and or at least this was all he could remember of it when he was a grown-up.

11

CHAPTER TWO

Chapter 2

Ali's experiences growing up in the East

When finally the time came for Ali to go to school, he soon realised that his whole life was beginning to change dramatically. First of all, he had to have his hair cut; he had long straight hair coming down to his shoulders. When their neighbourhood Barber started cutting his hair, Ali became so sad, he sobbed begging for his hair not to be cut but to no avail. The situation became so bad that the Barber commented that it was as if "they wanted to cut his bird" and was quite bewildered in astonishment. His father ordered him to sit still for his hair to be cut and apologised to the Barber for the embarrassment. It was simply quite unimaginable for a boy to go to school with such long hair, having long hair was only for the girls. So after years of impatiently waiting and wishing to go to school, it was already turning out to prove to be the start of painful changes and a great disappointment.

Ali could remember how particular was his school days, children gatherings of all ages, always so noisy and crowded. When the school bell rang all would gather in the school yard in lines, one line for each class and then a boy usually of the oldest age at school would say the morning prayers and after that the school's Head Teacher would announce any special event of the day and then everyone would quietly go to their classes, line after line. In every class while waiting for the teacher to come, there was a complete chaos. There was a lot of joking, shouting, hitting and swearing and no one would mind any of it. Ali was attending a Boys only school and such were the state of things when he was a boy. He could remember all jokes were allowed and every kind of swearing word was common. However things were getting serious only when there was a nasty swearing, a deliberate mention of someone's sister or mother. Everyone's mother or sister was very sacred and mentioning them without justified reason could lead to endless fights and grudges. Everyone needed to defend the fact that he was from clean, respectable family and any hint of the contrary was a serious blasphemy. One's mother, sister and of course later on one's wife, daughter and to some extent even one's country were considered to be one's "Namous". One's Namous needed to be defended from blasphemy and attack at all cost.

The concept of Namous was not something that would be taught at school but something that was passed from generation to generation. It was of most inherent nature in the society; it was that zest with which everyone was fighting with the slightest mention of the smallest unsuitable comment or gesture against their Holy. This zest was called "Gheirat". As these concepts were practised through generations, they were commonly accepted and expected through the society. Hence for example, if there was proof of someone having illegitimate relationship with a girl, there was expected to be serious trouble and the easiest solution would be that he would marry her. So if someone was interested in a girl, it was improper for him to directly approach her and the solution would be that first his family should contact her family for talks regarding marriage. However if the girl was directly approached she should ask that an approach to her family is required such that her hand would be requested from her father together with his blessing. Therefore, a girl would refuse to provoke for example by wearing Hejab and this refusal to provoke is known as Haya. This highly structured order in the society was possibly what originally necessitated the need for Hejab or covering for women. However Ali thought that girls were attractive no matter what they would wear, after all even he himself would wear his best dress on special occasions or on a day he felt simply nice and happy and would comb his hair to look his best, although he didn't genuinely generally care about his appearances. In the same way, he could see that girls were also trying to look their best under the Hejab and he thought they were quite successful at it. So nature always finds its ways and he was quite happy to notice that.

Ali remembered some Thursday nights, when he was asked to take Halva to the Mosque. The preparation of Halva by itself was quite an event as the sweet smell of roasting Flour would fill up the entire neighbourhood. After adding rose water, oil and sugar, his Mum would spread the mix on large dishes and would give some of the left over to Ali as she knew that he liked it very much. Ali loved the smell, taste and the texture of the hot mixture melting in his mouth and all his life still remembered and longed for those happy days. The smallest dish would stay at home, Ali then had to give a dish to each neighbourhood around. So after that he would take the largest dish and go to the mosque and offer it to all prayers one by one in both the male and female sections. He would take off his shoes entering the Mosque and then first go left through the long, heavy, thick black curtain and up the stairs which led to the ladies section. Even though he was just a child, he was well aware that entering there would not be allowed to him in just a couple of year's time and so he was very curious of how it would differ from the men's section and he was even slightly anxious. To his surprise, there was nothing unusual about that section, ladies sitting down, chatting to each other with their Chador dropped down round them. Chador is a kind of a Hejab, a long cloth used to cover the whole body except for the face, wrapped around loosely and held tightly with one hand below the chin. When he went up to the first lady to offer the Halva, it stirred quite a disturbance as she became aware of his presence and quickly grabbed her Chador pulling it over her head and asking Ali how old he was. He answered 12 and the answer seemed enough reassuring for the lady to drop back her Chador, smile politely, took the halva and gave her blessing to Ali and his family for the offering. Once started, things went on quite smoothly and so Ali was able to finish very quickly with both female and male sections. He knew that any left over would not be welcomed back home and so he gave all left over to the person who looks after the Mosque, received his blessings and asked him if he could keep the Halva dish for him, while he go for praying. The man was really impressed with his manners and his great effort at such young age and was very happy to help Ali.

Ali had been taught how to pray and do the fasting and also all the procedures required to be done prior to pray and fasting. So before the praying one needed to do the cleaning procedure called Vozou and keep clean until the praying would start and certainly until the praying was over. Vozou is a cleaning procedure necessary to be done prior to praying and is done by mainly cleaning face, hands, head and feet briefly with water or with clean sand in the absence of water. He also had learnt that it would be a very good practice to go to the toilet before any preparation to pray, because otherwise and just in case, if he needed to go to the toilette, then he had to do all the procedure all over again. This was because going to the toilette would void the preparations to pray. He also read and researched different religious books to do all the procedures as best as he could. However during his research, it became apparent to him that most procedures of cleanliness in fact were referring to a married life and explained everything for the people of the age. Although he was still a child, he still prayed and fasted all the same to accompany the other members of the family and to learn. Although he was not of age yet and knew that he was under no obligation to pray or Fast, but he still wanted to experience the difficulties and be prepared for when he grows up.

Ali was known to be really an expert in praying and even knew extra verses or suras that were interchangeable in the pray. He was taught to read and correctly pronounce Arabic and knew many suras of The Holy

Quran by heart and always boasted about how well he had learnt all the details publicly. Following the completion of his errand and knowing that it would be late when he eventually would be finished with his task, he had done all the preparations necessary for his praying well in advance. He had worn a clean dress, had done Vozou and had been very careful to keep clean for the praying. Although he was very tired, he was already in the best place to pray. It simply seemed best practice to pray despite the fact that he still was not of age and didn't have to do it, he knew that he still possibly had some time to pray and that the Halva dish would be safe. So he did his praying in companion of some late comers who were now praying scattered here and there or were hurriedly coming and starting to pray while he was still praying. Even to date, Ali could vividly remember that day, that praying gave him the impression and feeling of belonging to a wider community, people he was seeing for the first time. Yet, although it was the first time that he was doing something on his own and all alone, it felt quite good. He felt accepted, alive and grown up because how people were behaving to him was like how people were treating his father on few occasions that his father had taken Ali to Mosque with him. He really felt very special when the few people finishing their prayers here and there were briefly coming to each other and to him to shake hands and to wish him "May their prayers be accepted by the God". That for him was the proof that he had learnt everything well such that no one had noticed any of his possible mistakes that is if he had made any, and he felt real satisfied with himself. Then he remembered it was getting real late, so he retrieved the dish and got on the way off quickly back home.

On his way back home that evening and in a quiet road, Ali found a bundle of money on the pavement. Life does offer situations at times that require discretion and immediate action and it was there for him this time. All he needed to do was to grab the money and put it in his pocket, it was his lucky day. However he didn't do that, his first reaction was to look around him to see if he sees the person who possibly could have accidentally dropped the money, but it was very silent and no-one to be seen. So he took a closer look, it was considerable amount of money on the ground, surely whoever lost it, would come back to search for it. Ali found himself in the biggest dilemma he ever had in his life. He was told not to touch anything that is does not belong to him and in addition he knew that he should never tell a lie, may be not even a white one and so he decided to leave the money where it is and just to walk off. This was because he couldn't find a way to justify himself to his family, taking the money. Also he couldn't even use the money if he were to keep it a secret. Ali was thinking of the numerous things he could have bought or done with the money but also dreaded that he will be needed to explain where he got the money from. He was afraid of the fact that he might be doing something which was considered to be wrong. He was taught to always give to the poor, be kind to everyone, carry heavy shopping for a total stranger of old age and give up his seat for a person in need in a busy bus. He was told, he should take extreme care of anything trusted to him and that he should be true to his word. He actually did turn out to be a very traditional, Gheirati, boy as well, which meant that he was very particular on his mother and his sisters and thought very highly of his responsibility to his sacred, Namous. Ali felt his utmost duty that he needed to protect all his sacred from bad eyes and bad intentions at all times. He wanted to be true to all customs and traditions known to him that had passed to him from generation to generation before him and he wanted to have his conscience at ease that he was doing everything right, every time. However no matter how hard he fought with his inner self, he wasn't sure if he was doing the right thing leaving the money behind. Surely, it was his own greatest ever dilemma to date, the only matter it seemed that he had never received any kind of instructions of how to precede. However, none the least, it was the most important one that he needed to make a decision about it on his own, and quickly, he needed rational thinking, judgement and decision making. He even considered taking the money and giving it to the poor, but in the end he decided to just walk away and go home; leaving the money untouched because in this way whatever happened would not be his responsibility any more. Walking away, he kept looking back over his shoulder still unsure if he was doing the right thing. Further up the road and before he reached home, Ali this time found a piece of bread on the pavement, Ali didn't give much notice and walked on.

Then a man, an old man passing by saw the piece of bread exposed to the street's dirt, he picked the bread up, kissed it and put it somewhere high so that it may be used by a bird or an animal. When the man noted Ali watching him, he gently looked back and gave him a kind glance, but said nothing. Ali knew that you should never waste food, but the stance of the man simply shocked him because the man was simply obsessed with saving the bread. When he reached home, he never mentioned anything about his experiences or his feelings of the day. He just kept his silence as his house was always so busy that no questions were asked unless there was a problem.

Ali still remembered those times that he spent with his Mum everyday and all the time as a child, especially during mornings. When everyone would leave home in the mornings, his Mum would take him and go out to do the household shopping. They would go to the neighbourhood bakery, grocery and sometimes take the bus to their local market, bazaar. Mum also used to have women from the neighbourhood coming over. Most of his Mum's gatherings were when Dad was at work; ladies would come for tea and biscuit at their house and chat along. Dad's friends' gatherings would be usually during the evening, Mum and sometimes even his sisters would be present but they would wear chador or head scarves, sit at a corner and talk not so frequently. They would also be tasked to provide tea, biscuits or serve dinner to the guests according to the occasion. Mum's friends were mostly unknown to Dad and he would know of their existence only when Mum would explain that such and such people had come and a summary of who they were and what had been said. Dad would hardly ever comment Mum's friends, Dad's friends however were mostly known to Mum because she would be present during the whole gatherings. Although little she talked with anyone, but Mum had clear knowledge of all Dad's friends and their business, so as such had her own personal opinion regarding them and would even comment and give her opinion about them to Dad. However Mum usually only ever commented Dad's friends only when the gatherings were over or during the following day of the gatherings in her discussions with Dad.

Family gatherings would be somehow different; chador and scarf would still possibly be worn if the family was distant but everything was more relaxed in the close family gatherings. Although these gatherings were an opportunity for Ali to get to know girls of his age and play with them, he felt too shy in their presence and hardly properly talked to them. Sometimes they played hide and seek or other games in groups but that was it. During those short encounters, he was treating girls exactly like boys but he was aware that they behaved very differently and was curious to get to know them better. However the play time would soon be over and the next time he would have a chance to play with the girls would depend on when the next family or friends gathering would be and such gatherings were seldom and long in between.

Such was Ali's childhood and he remembered himself to be a happy child with no real care in the world but life never stays the same for ever, sooner or later the awkward age of puberty comes for every child. If only he were told what was destined to be happening to him, he might possibly would have been able to enjoy his puberty as any other periods of his life because life is so beautiful and you have to enjoy every moment of it. However, he was not prepared for such natural cause mishap that was about to happen to him. He knew nothing of his body changes during puberty and the implications that came with reaching the puberty age.

During his childhood years and before his puberty, he used to be taken care of by his Mum and Dad. Mum would comb his head, cream his hands and body and listen and attend to all his wishes. Dad would bath him every time before he himself bathed and attended to his homework enquiries. Just before his teenage years, he was tasked to do all his cleaning and taking care of himself. Ali still remembered how hard he was to himself at early age because of some silly boyish notions such as boys need to be rough, and so he considered even using a hand cream as girly stuff such so that when his hands' severely dried skin would splinter and was slightly bleeding; he would hide it from his sisters, rather than using a hand cream.

Looking back on his teenage years; Ali couldn't do anything but sigh with heavy heart. Every time he remembered his teenage years, he was dazed by his experience of going through such horrible years alone and miserable. Oh how he wished there would have been some kind of guidance to conduct him through the changes every child goes through during those years. It's at the least awkward and embarrassing, for girls, he thought the changes might be even frightening. He was sure there would have been some kind of preparation, warning given to his sisters by his Mum, he later remembered silent secretive whispers between his Mum and sisters but what about him? Who was supposed to warn him about the changes about to happen to him in order for him to be aware and prepared. If only he could ask someone or read somewhere about it. Life went on as before for everyone he knew, even his friends at school, it seemed everything as usual for everyone around him. Of course everyone noted his voice changing and his moustache to start appearing and his height and body structure changing. The only thing that seemed to worry his family was that he would complete the manhood procedure to grow his full beard; no one seemed to like men with a thin beard.

His body changes however were a complete nuisance to him, his first reactions were to try and hide his symptoms and shy away of every hint or mention of his adolescence. Actually for many years later and thinking back, he was shocked to find out for how long he would continue the same behaviour. It was as if all his life he was a victim of two huge forces inside him, one was pushing him towards girls and another shying away from them. He remembered how at the time and for a short time he even resolved to just forget about the whole thing and just pray the symptoms he was experiencing would just stop. Somehow he knew his life would never be the same because there would be no return to childhood. It wasn't that he didn't want to embrace difficulties associated with change to adulthood. He actually even enjoyed to finally be considered as a grown up but he didn't know how to cope with the changes happening to him. He didn't know if everyone was going through exactly the same changes happening to him and if so how they were coping. He also couldn't find any books to get some answers and was too shy to ask anyone close to him. It was just that he simply wished he could live independent and free of the actual need to be with anyone, that is if he was still not of the age to get married, everything seemed to be simpler before his teenage years.

Even before his adolescence years, Ali remembered having loads of questions as a child, but the answer to nearly all his questions was that you will know once you grow up and come to the age. Especially when he asked a question concerning girls, his answer was sometimes even a complete silence. It was as if he had not spoken at all or the words were never heard. Day by day, his questions were becoming more and more of the grown up nature, mostly because he was gradually and slowly welcomed to learn about grown up issues by listening to religious lessons or reading religious books but as such without proper support from the grown-ups in explaining the details. For example he knew that he was Mahram to his immediate family, that meant as a general rule his Mum and sisters were not required to wear Hejab in his presence. Mahram is the condition of allowed intimacy and it's granted by birth such as for example the intimacy between a mother and his son. However the same word is also used to describe the intimacy between husband and wife as granted by marriage. In this respect, there was detailed description of the limitations of two persons being Mahram to each other due to natural intimacy in the books; however in the same books there seemed to be no barrier or restrictions between a husband and his wife for that matter. He found this hard to understand as a child. His question was simply how it could be that with an unknown girl that he sees for the first time, there would be allowed such unlimited mutual intimacy between them and much more than the intimacy allowed between him and his own nearest family. How was it that a girl could suddenly become Mahram to him only because of the marriage process? Or why should girls even be required to wear Hejab in the presence of a man at all?

Although these questions were unanswered, he was taught manners at early age. He was told that he should shake hands only with his right hand, wear a watch on his left and be neat and clean all the time. For example even when he grew older, it didn't matter if he grew a beard or moustache but as long as it looked trimmed and cared for it was fine. It was most important that he should always have respect for the elderly, to listen carefully to their words, to get up when they enter the room and to always be polite when addressing them. Also he needed to be aware of the disabled people, like for example give up his seat in a bus for an old person or a pregnant lady. He should never lie, and his word of honour, let alone for his promise, should be as if the word is written in stone. He was taught that it was not good to accept Tavoun for anything lost or broken and indeed it was to a person's credit if he could declare that he has neither ever given, nor ever taken Tavoun in his life. Tavoun is an amount of money or anything else, given to you in replacement for something damaged, broken or lost. For example, if your friend accidentally looses or breaks your favourite ruler, Tavoun would be the amount of money given to you equal to the value of the ruler, or another same or similar ruler given, in order to replace it. However if the ruler was to be broken or lost intentionally, then it's a different matter and should be replaced or paid for by the person breaking or loosing it.

Ali was taught all the above which were things that were quite tangible stuff and he could understand them except for the requirement of not accepting the Tavoun. He could understand the concept of Tavoun, but its non acceptance, he could not quite justify as a child and again he was given no reasoning for not accepting Tavoun, it was simply advised that it is just how it should be.

However there was also the intangible stuff, when the intangible stuff was explained to him, he was completely bewildered and perplexed. Intangible stuff was things such as for example the concept of the "destiny" or otherwise known as "Tagdir" or "Sarnevesht". It was certainly more difficult to describe but in short was described to him that the "destiny" could be explained as again almost a magical outcome to an event, or equally successive occurrence of certain unexpected events that eventually would shape the future of a person, or would change the outcome of an event. Another example of an intangible thing was the concept of the "eye" or "Cheshm". It was explained to him that the "eye" could be explained as almost a magical interaction of people between themselves where the extreme desire of a person towards other people's looks or possessions, could eventually have an unexplained negative affect on them. This was to be taken almost as a phenomenon rather than a scientific happening and again no explanation given. Last but not least was the intangible concept of Taqas which has been translated in English as Karma. Taqas could be explained as the unexplained influence of your actions on your fate.

It was weird but even as a child; Ali could somehow find an invisible correlation between the concepts connecting Tagdir, Tavoun, Tagas and the Eye. So back to the ruler example: there would be two scenarios, one that his friend breaks his ruler on purpose and so must replace it, his friend's bad intentions has the consequence of paying a penalty which could remotely be translated as Tagas. However in the second scenarios, that the ruler breaks accidentally, it is purely the destiny or the tagdir of his ruler to be broken, if so, then it was not his friend's fault to break his ruler. It was the hands of the destiny setting his friend to somehow make the break of his ruler to happen, for example he moves his book which pushes the ruler off the table and the ruler falls down and breaks. Now if we assume all that to be valid, then we could see why he shouldn't receive a Tavoun for the ruler, simply because it was not really his friends fault. Lastly if Ali decided not to believe in tagdir and tavoun and so he would claim compensation for the broken ruler and gets it, then we have to deal with the "eye" concept. In this way, Ali's friend would have an eye for the money he must give to Ali a Tavoun because the friend would believe unfair to compensate for the ruler as he didn't break it intentionally. Hence Ali could justify how it was considered not good to accept Tavoun.

Another example of how to explain Taqas, Ali could only think about Taqas and it's translation as Karma only in its negative form and possibly unlike it's translation as Karma; he could not relate Taqas to anything good happening. He could only imagine Taqas as a worldly punishment as a result of wicked actions or intentional mischievous and unfair practices towards others. Ali could think of the story of the Shepherd who used to sell his milk diluted with water over many years, only to find his sheep strangled by flood many years later, as his Taqas. In his childish mind Ali only could think of all the little amount of water every time milk was diluted, accumulated over the years in shape of a flood.

Destiny would also be a weird roll out of different unexpected happenings that would eventually influence or even determine the outcome of something. It sometimes seems as if no matter how hard you try to achieve something, everything is against it happening and there seem to be nothing else to do but to try again and again for it. An example would be like missing a train home when you unexpectedly run into a friend while running for it and having to wait for the next train. It would actually have been wiser to just stop running, spend the time waiting for the next train with your friend and be determined to catch the next train as soon as you accidentally meet a long lost friend. This seemingly small delay in the journey has domino effect which affects other people as well, like which taxi driver will eventually serve you when you reach at your destination or who you will meet once in your neighbourhood.

Ali was told that the intangible stuff were not to be mixed with mere superstition. As a child, he was completely confused about these concepts and because he could not distinguish between the superstition and likely intangible facts, he decided to forget or rather to disregard the whole concept altogether. He made his own discretion about things but when he ran into problems, Ali sought advice from an elderly. Despite all this, he could admit he was sometimes giving way to the superstition to get the better of a difficult situation, especially when he was doing important things for the very first time. The kind of superstition that required him for example to stop or postpone whatever he intended to do, if he sneezed. He didn't know the exact reason behind it but he was told that it was considered bad or it was the wrong timing and so if he was to start immediately after sneezing, that something would go wrong in his endeavour. He didn't believe it to be true but he considered waiting for a few seconds and thinking over all the details of what he was doing once more, couldn't hurt, just in case and to be on the safe side. Another example of mere superstition would be to believe in bad luck when you see a black cat. There were rumours that this was true specially if you see a black cat early in the day but even with his young mind he could never see any relation between bad luck and any cat, that is because he loved animals and refused to relate them to any bad thing at all. However, his justification for the acceptance of any superstition at all, was that once a society deeply believed in any concept, it might come true. The problem is that if any society must believe in any indefinite concept such as the destiny, the eye, taqas or tavoun, then unfortunately that society might naturally be more prone to believing in the superstition as well, or at least be mindful of them.

On the other hand, Ali was fascinated about the Zoroastrianism religion of Ancient Persia. The religion of "Pendare nik, Goftare nik and Kerdare nik", that is: "thinking good thoughts, saying good words and doing good deeds". It seemed to him the best ever concept of running everyday life. Ali sincerely believed these three simple ways of running anybody's everyday life, very simply depicted the way to be a true human. Just imagine a world where everyone just tried to think of only how to be positive in life and help one another, everybody opened their mouth only just to express one's positive suggestion for improvements or words that were initiated purely out of deep feelings of love and to explain one's reasoning of it. Finally doing good deeds where everyone only took steps to carry out the good thoughts, alone or in agreement with other same minded individuals and all in order to achieve mutual happiness and a better life for everyone.

In this way, the ideas of different people could lead to laws or decisions that are taken in a democratic way where meetings are brainstorming sessions and the validity of Pendare nik, Goftare nik and Kerdare nik concept is being verified in every decision or every occasion. This certainly would have been and could potentially be a stepping stone in progress and success for the whole mankind in the world. Zoroastrianism was a belief that Ali was taught early in life and he literally had fallen in love with it as a child and no matter how much he pondered the concept for a fault, he couldn't find anything that could go wrong with a society, if every single person truly understood, believed and was determined to apply the concept to his or her everyday life.

It was only when Ali was being hurt by the actions of other people, or their words, that he was having difficulty with Pendare Nik which is thinking good thoughts. It was difficult to feel sympathy with people who were being selfish and had no respect for others. Still worse, how could he sympathise with people who were trying to hurt him because of their excessive greed, it was going beyond himself. But then he realised that in this way, then others behaviour to him was against Zoroastrianism belief. He couldn't change others but he could do all in his might to confront the greedy people. He decided even to forgive in order for him to move forward with his life. He had realised that when you cling to a bad, rotten past, or hold a grudge against someone, it holds you back. Ali believed that the mere thought of getting back to another person for the damage they have caused to him, should only be justified by the amount of harm it was going to do back to himself and the severity of the matter. It was considering the amount of his precious time and effort that would be spent for the whole process, against numerous other positive things that he could have done at the same amount of time. He needed to ask himself every time if it was worth it. Also if he had already done whatever he could logically do to stop the greedy people or reverse the loss they had caused him, was it worth it to pursue them and make them pay for their wickedness or he should just get on with his life. So in most cases, his decision was to be temporarily forgiving but not to forget. The history of people's actions towards you and the history of your own actions should be remembered because you can only learn from your old mistakes and if you forget, then you are prone to do the same mistakes again. Also the greedy people might surely try their nasty trick on other people.

Although it was possibly quite easy to find books to look into how Zoroastrianism punished outlaws, he left further investigation into the religion for when he could himself go to a region where people still had the religion for further research. Later in his life, when Ali knew the concepts of micro and macro economics and their interrelation, he realised that Zoroastrianism basic instructions address only in micro or at the individual level but there seemed to be nothing in macro scale. He could not be sure and wished he could know more about the religion. After all it was an ancient religion for smaller and local societies of the time and possibly not so applicable to today's life, but Ali honoured and respected the religion all the same.

III

CHAPTER THREE

Chapter 3

Ali's difficulties as a grown up now living in the West

Ali immigrated to the West at a young age. He was optimistic about the change, he didn't know exactly what awaits him but hoped that he could settle nicely and have a better life. He knew of other people who had immigrated before him and all were very successful with good jobs and running a happy life. At first he was confronted with the immigration laws of his hosting country.

Every country has rules which are different for its residents and non-resident members coming from a foreign country and that's only natural. So as an immigrant, Ali expected his endeavour to be extremely stressful and was prepared for any difficulties along the way. He accepted to have hardship in his immigration and suffer in order to adapt to the new reality. After all he had come to a different continent, there were different ways of thinking and doing things here than in his own country. There were different culture and people with different believes, different life values which all lead to different behaviour. The difference in the standards of living between his developing country and the West was his main reason to immigrate. He had friends who were victims of Human Rights issues such as being discriminated by their home country for their belief, religion or political opinions and also friends who were victims of different wars, all from different developing countries around the world. Ali could see that the number of immigrants was getting unbearable for any western country, making it more and more difficult for the West to accept everyone. It had become apparent that it was practically impossible to get a tourist or a student visa any-more and so he was glad that he had made it. At the same time he also soon realised that there were consequences for being born somewhere else and be a foreigner in another continent. That is in its simplest form you needed a residence permit to continue to legally stay and a work permit to be able to work without any restrictions.

Upon his arrival, Ali was told that he had to wait for his residence permit to be decided; in the meantime he had no work permit and couldn't officially work. He remembered feeling that his "waiting time" would have been probably OK for weeks and months but certainly not for years and years. He felt all his desire, hope, wishful thinking and energy to do things and have a better life going to waste day after day, week after week and year after year. All he could see was other people enjoying their lives, couples of his own age, hand in hand in the park, people buying what they need or desire from the shops. There were also even different programs from the European Union which were in place to help the residence of every EU country to get to know each other better and enjoy life even more. However none of it was applied to Ali. He was born in the East and of course this was the biggest mistake of his life and again of course he could get cash in hand job. In fact, Ali indeed did have cash in hand part time jobs while his immigration status was under consideration. A job in a compatriot's shop, just to provide for example to have that small amount of money for coffee with a friend, however the work offered was of lowest profile, often in restaurant's kitchen or pastry shops with long hours of work and very low pay. The work under such conditions was better than nothing because now he could get one decent pair of acceptable clothing and some money to use in order to be experiencing life like his western friends even if short lived and at great cost. So he would happily pay the equivalent of his days work, twelve hours each day work of his Friday, Saturday and Sunday to watch a film with friends and would walk back home if he missed the last bus late at night because Taxis were too expensive for him. So he managed to live a normal life even during his "waiting time" years but he was not happy. It simply felt too much, that is, he needed to spend so much time and effort to get a fraction of the salary others would get for doing the same or similar job. His "waiting time" took ages and anything to do with the local Home Office was a lengthy and sometimes very expensive procedure. Having your residence permit in date was an obligatory requirement that was required for him but not for his Western friends because they were born locally. All his Western friends sympathised with him and helped him as much as possible, he was deeply thankful to them and didn't know what he would do without them but somehow at the same time, he wanted no charity from anyone.

Ali had to wait for many years before he was given permission to reside and work without any restrictions. Thinking back, he despised every minute of those never ending years when he was young and he had loads of energy, enthusiasm, ideas and dreams but couldn't legally do anything. Although he had so many friends, deep within, he felt poor, miserable and lonely. Ali considered himself to be just a very young man who was deprived of what other people of his own age were doing. Young people of his age were all around him, they were all enjoying themselves, living their happy life and doing things he had always only wished and dreamed of doing himself. Things like swimming, going for ski to different countries in winter time or even things as simple as going to the cinema and eating some popcorn while watching a film. The fact was that he didn't have enough money to even do such simple things as going to the movies. Swimming would have been nice but he didn't know how to swim properly and in fact, nearly none of his refugee friends were confident swimmers. Mostly because it was not something that you would learn in the East as a child, except for the children of very rich families or for the regions where fishing or working with boats were part of their everyday life.

He sincerely believed that there should be a "Waiting" cap imposed by some kind of a global entity to manage the immigration systems in all different Western countries. This was because the average waiting time for all foreigners to get settled was exceptionally high. Ali felt it was sheer devastating as a young man to have to wait for his permit to work for years and years. Years and years of living in poverty, Ali had to spend the best years of his life waiting to be permitted to work. Only if he would have been born in the West, then he wasn't required to have a work permit or to suffer. Ali couldn't help but to think that he was being legally discriminated because of where he was born but no one seemed to notice or care. The general idea he was getting from the locals and people from his own country that had settled status was that he was lucky to be there. He had to consider people like him who were drowning every day in order to reach where he was. Also the situation seemed to be getting worse and worse with many more people immigrating by the day. Employees in his local Home office would point out that he could leave whenever he wanted and go back to the country he originated from. So any complaints of how long it's taking for settlement was out of question. Considering the fact that he had to choose to escape from his own country, he also despised the politicians running his birth country in the East. Those Politicians were wicked, unscrupulous, ruthless and ignorant opportunists who somehow got together in the position of Power and formed a government. They were the reason why he had to flee his own country in the first place and live somewhere he didn't belong and felt unwanted. It was not only himself that he was thinking about, he was also thinking about the millions of his compatriots who were suffering everyday as a result of still living in his birth country. He was also thinking about his other compatriots who had fled and were experiencing similar difficulties in other countries. Ali could not decide how his home country politicians should ever be punished one day. He just decided he couldn't go back yet whatever the cost, he needed to stay where he was and try to make the best of it.

It was now years since Ali had travelled to the West and finally one day he was given the acceptance of his refugee status by his host country and then eventually his Western citizenship and he was allowed to live like everyone else and more importantly have the same rights as everyone else around him. He was glad that he had achieved his highest ever desire of his lifetime that he could ever imagine would come true one day. However at the same time, it was to his own surprise and horror to realise that deep within him, he felt no joy of finally getting his long desired citizenship. He started to feel absolute and sheer fear. There was so much time wasted in order to get to what other people around him had as usual everyday life and granted to them since their birth. He was missing so much and now that officially he was one of them, Ali wondered how on Earth he could ever compete with all other young people of his age. After all, he was only just allowed to live properly. Despite all this, Ali was amazed to remember as to how many things that he had ever desired actually somehow came true for him, getting his naturalisation as a Western citizen was possibly one of the most important ones.

Life was full of opportunities and it was not always clear what is the best choice, but nearly always Ali had some kind of an opportunity to get whatever he desired. Sometimes all that was required of him was only to reach out and grab the opportunity, a simple action, a word, a touch or a nod would have been sufficient. He could remember leaving the bundle of money untouched while walking in the streets one day as a child and he very well knew he certainly would bend down and grab the bundle of money if it was to happen to him again, now. In the same way, Ali couldn't help but wonder how many such hidden characteristics of his old self he still did carry within him. That is, he truly didn't know how many of his old notions that belonged to another culture, he still clung to within himself. As far as he could remember he had sometimes grabbed an opportunity and sometimes hadn't. When he had not grabbed an opportunity, it was not because he couldn't see the opportunity but mostly because of the way he was brought up. For some of his lost opportunities he felt sorry, for some even today he felt indifferent and for some other lost opportunities he just considered as his fate in life or tagdir. It was his philosophy that his destiny has been to loose one opportunity which should change the course of his life forever. Whether he was able to recognise every opportunity as it revealed itself to him or he just let go of the opportunity didn't even seem to matter any more. The issue now seemed to be broader than this. The big question now seemed only to be how his inherent culture, that is his old societies' accepted standards, were affecting his behaviour now. Therefore, how the Western people around him observed his decision making, judged and understood him. What would have been considered completely acceptable behaviour back in his own country, might as well be wrong or strange behaviour in the West.

He started from scratch, found a job and rented a house; he turned his house into a home which was quite cosy and in accordance to his taste. He learnt how to cook the traditional, delicious dishes of his home country as much as he could but if he was lazy or short of time, he would just go to the closest restaurant with food from his land in the city he lived in, even though it would still be a long journey to that restaurant. He was happy living in the West because he was a free man, he had everything he needed and he was successful in his job with a very good salary. He would take the public transport to work, he knew the exact timetable of every bus, train and underground tube and so had good, fast commute to any place he wanted from his home. For his leisure, he had got a sport car, good, easy life. The most important thing was that he had achieved a routine in his life. Having a routine is excellent but somehow you don't realise the passage of time. Days, months and years were passing without any specific plan or any specific goal in his life.

One weekend, Ali was enjoying a lazy day, not knowing what to do.

In a beautiful day when you do what you want and take time to treat yourself, it's a heavenly experience. As it was a sunny day, Ali decided to go to a nearby park for jogging. It was then that he realised how all his days were nearly the same, it didn't really matter if he had something to do or not. It didn't even matter if he had money or not. It had seemed that all his days were passing without any plan, day after day of going to work, endless futile small chores at home and thinking what to do each day. He remembered he couldn't even enjoy jogging or even have fun with his friends any more like before. Whatever he did, it was time wasting. His life style was futile because he had nothing to do and lived only to treat himself. His whole life seemed to have become pointless. Ali then started to travel globally, to take to tourism and go to cruises to far off beautiful destinations which were quite enjoyable and kept him busy. However he soon realised that he knew nothing of the people he met during his journeys. They were all kinds of people with smiles and polite gestures serving him in restaurants and hotels all over the world. Native people who were serving him wherever he went, he had no idea how they were coming to work, their everyday problems, their main diet and how they survived, making a living everyday Even Ali's visit to every countries historic monuments were pure superficial. He felt he was learning nothing of the civilisation he was visiting, how the local people were attracted to the specific location and chose to call it home. So what was the point of travelling, what could he possibly achieve by going to visit so many different places. Looking back, on one occasion, Ali would clearly remember the faces of the local salesmen running after him, begging him to buy just anything from them, showing him their products. He could remember those poor men and their endeavour to survive, more vividly than the dip he had in the beach at the same poor country he visited. Ali was filled with sadness remembering it but somehow calmed himself thinking that it would have been impossible to buy all their products and it would have not been practical to make them all happy. Most importantly Ali realised that he had spent several years of his life travelling and had not attended to the real problems in his life. After wasting so many years of his life enjoying himself, he now had to look for girls. So many years older girls than what he would have found, if he had decided to settle and have a family as soon as it was possible at the time. That is as soon as he was eligible to live and work as a western naturalised citizen. The most important question seemed to be if marriage was the answer to all his problems. Surely he could have been married; he could have treated his wife and himself and also had travelled the world together with his partner. He didn't know if then he would have got any satisfaction in his life. However, now it was too late, years had passed and now he was not happy deep inside no matter what he did. He knew money comes and goes and he had never been really upset with anything in his life. His income had been sometimes a little less and other times a little bit more. Material things in life were there to make ends meet. The important thing seemed to be what he really achieved with passage of time.

He had loads of friends and acquaintances but no family, most of his friends who had settled immigration status like himself had similar life problems and experiences with him. They only differed as to how they had immigrated, how long they had to wait for their settlement status, where they worked, when and where they learnt the local language and how frequently they visited their home country. Occasionally on weekends Ali and his friends would get together for a drink or go to a concert or to an event. During their getting together times, they would update each other of the latest news of their home-country. They would also discuss any changes to the laws of the country they were living in and what was happening in each others lives. Sometimes they would just simply go for a walk in the park or to each others houses for coffee. Ali now did have an excellent life but despite his happiness of living in the West, deep within himself, he felt lonely. Ali needed someone whom to share his life with. Years had passed, but as long as he could remember nothing major had changed in his life or the lives of his acquaintances or friends for that matter. They also shared the same problem of loneliness with him, in fact the older he got, the more alone and miserable he felt and he could see that the same was true with all his friends.

At the very beginning, when he had first arrived to the West, the initial vivid differences of how people dressed and lived in the West to what he was used to in his own country was nothing less than a shock. During his journey of coming to the West, he was under such pressure and felt such great anxiety about his journey that he somehow he ignored everything else. However shortly after that and sure enough, the new reality was there whenever he left home, he had done it; he had immigrated to the West. Girls would sit next to him in a bus or talk to him in a park, girls that he liked and would very much have wanted to get to know them better. However he found himself not to be able to utter a word to talk to them but maybe at most a faint hello. If the girl asked him a question, he would suffice at just answering the question and walk away. Ali couldn't understand what problem he was experiencing because he did not know himself to be shy and he knew enough English to make a simple conversation.

Ever since he had travelled to the West, he was thinking about how he could truly get to know a girl, live with her and eventually marry her and have a family. Yet there was one big problem, he felt that he knew nothing of the opposite sex, of the way women thought, responded to their needs, their reactions to fear, hope, desire or despair. It was funny, women were all around him all his life but still had become the greatest mystery all the same. After all, how could he possibly know anything about women while during all the time that he lived in the East, basically the earliest years of his life, he was completely separated of the other half of the world's population through no faults of his own. His society was separated, any communications with girls was limited, all schools were separated from early age, even the hobbies and how their time was spent was different for boys and girls. Looking back he thought that he had been treated unfairly as a child even by his nearest family and elders because his every attempt to get an answer to his questions regarding girls back then was somehow overlooked. However it was not really their fault as anything Sex related or even the word Sex was a taboo in the Eastern society, at the time of his childhood or maybe even now. They would say, "He will know when the time comes and he will be of the age". It was really what he now named as the society's invisible great wall which separated men from women and boys from girls in his homeland. Just like the black curtain that he once simply slide away as a child and entered the women's section in the Mosque to deliver the Halva, Ali could see that there was actually an invisible wall separating the whole Eastern society. However this very strong but invisible wall is very difficult to just simply slide away once you were a grown up. As a grown up, you simply had to learn to be agile and abide by the society rules. Men behaving and talking quite differently in the presence of a lady or a girl, for example men wouldn't swear or spit or be impolite in their presence and then switch back to their normal own self once a lady or a girl is out of site. Such difference in behaviour between when men are alone and when a girl would be between them might be common even in the West, however the extent of the difference is not the same. Even as a child he could see that invisible wall in everyday life. He could remember seeing and feeling that invisible wall in all gatherings, everywhere and all the time.

In the West it is different, boys and girls are living together in a natural environment and away from any kind of legal restrictions. He thought his Western colleagues, friends and acquaintances were so much ahead of him regarding a couple's relationship. Ali tried lengthy discussions of how his Western friends viewed girls but to no avail, he was not getting the answer that he needed. He would say that he was shy with girls and would ask for their advice. He found it was a popular subject, one that everyone knew himself as an expert who could give a precise account of how exactly to behave with girls. However Ali was absolutely shocked that on the majority of occasions, it was the numerous accounts of success with girls each friend could boast about or the description of the best tricks that could soften the hardest girls to be your friend in no time that would become the main subject of the conversation. Other, more mature friends would just suffice to say that it's something that just comes with time and will come by itself. That is once Ali himself was ready which sounded plausible, but was not the answer he was looking for. Ali felt absolutely disappointed. It was not the fact that he considered it wrong to learn about good techniques of approaching girls or didn't want to wait in order to get to know some girls better. It was simply disappointing to learn that there were men who were doing it as a hobby. In this way, they were betraying the trust in the society and what happens to a girl that truly likes the pretending man and who is looking for her partner in life. Was that all you could learn by having a usual childhood? What was wrong? Was there a fault with the society or was it simply the Human nature? Ali was devastated by the question that had come to his mind but he could not think of an answer. It was actually quite confusing, if the Western boys were like that, how could he trust the girls? Marriage had suddenly seemed like entering into a never ending crying game where you need to be suspicious of everyone around you. But what about the trust, living in good and bad times together and living happily ever after? Surely he could somehow find his pair in the West one day.

Ali was thinking that if he was in his homeland how easy it might have been for him to marry and have a family of his own. He was a successful young man with a good job and a good income, the way he was now, would be considered as "ready" for marriage back in his homeland. That is to say that if he had the same age, job, income and social standing he was having here in the West back in his homeland now, he would have been considered a perfect candidate for marriage back there. Actually, better said, he would have been urged to marry and make a family of his own by all his relatives and friends. He could choose a girl in between the ones that he met and joked with everyday, would ask her about her feelings for him and then would have requested his family to reveal his sincere feelings and good intentions to the girl's family. Back home marriage in itself was much easier because it was based in position of trust. Everything was arranged in between the families and the procedure was conducted according to certain traditions which ran in the society. It was known that the young couple are just getting together and it is supposed that the boy and the girl both are quite inexperienced in the ways of love. The girl knew that his boy shouldn't be a Casanova and the boy actually expected that in return for his years of accepting a solitude life in order to keep his purity, he was also getting a pure girl. Despite all hard work of the two families involved, marriage itself was so simple. The most important obvious outcome of the marriage was that the society was making solid building blocks of its next generation through simple steps. One "tested" procedure that was giving sure results for years, that is a procedure that would fuse together the boy and the girl with love and ensure prosperous marriage and loving children. Granted, it would not always work but it was the boys and the girl's first experience of love which in many cases would be the only one of their entire life.

First loves used to be arranged by families to happen at a very young age and possibly not that many years ago. It is definitely something that for today's living requirements of life is simply outdated for different possible reasons. One reason might be that the young generation needs to spend a long time to study or learn a skill in today's ever increasing demand for education in order to find a good job. This education is better done before marriage. However no doubt, the first experience of love is still possibly of greatest significance in anyone's life. Ali could think of a variety of songs that involve the mention of first love even in the Western culture.

However he was not in his homeland and was thinking about the best solution to his problem. The best solution that came to his mind was to get married with a foreign girl, to somehow find that other half that he had been longing for all his life. There were so many girls that he met on a daily basis and some of them actually knew him well and did show interest in him. However, he was so separated from women all his life that he felt he could never do this. Ali decided to marry locally but refused the Western boys techniques for approaching girls because he didn't agree with their ways and didn't want to be like them. Another solution came to his mind for giving himself more time for it all to happen naturally.

What if he would treat all girls exactly like boys, just like his childhood. He planned to become friends with them in order to get to know them better. In this way, it would be only a matter of time in order for him to get to know some girls and in time he could choose between them and reveal his real intentions to the right girl. This seemed like an excellent plan but in practice it didn't work. He couldn't know the exact problem but somehow being friendly with several girls at the same time didn't seem to work the way he planned it. Once he decided on a girl and thought it would be proper to reveal his feelings for her, but he found out that she was already engaged with her boyfriend who was away. Ali found that revealing your feelings to a girl only to realise she has got a distant boyfriend that she meets from time to time is a very heart breaking experience. Other times Ali would suddenly find out that a girl that he was seeing for some time has suddenly got together with another boy and isn't interested to spend time with him any more. Many times the girl's engagement with the other boy was quite short, like only a couple of weeks but then it was never again the same for him to look back at the girl in the same way, if nothing else, he felt rejected and hurt by her. No need to mention that meanwhile quite a lot of time did elapse in this way and Ali only found himself even lonelier than ever despite knowing and familiarising himself with so many people.

Ali then sought advice from some Western men who were already married as surely they knew exactly how to find the love of your life because they were already married. Here everyone considered his marriage to be lucky and had a different story to tell. However the basic rule seemed to be meeting someone and showing interest in them from the start. This somehow seemed to work, but he was confronted with yet another difficulty. If a girl recognised you as her possible pair, she immediately started to compare you with all the other boyfriends she had before you. Also even worse, it seemed that girls judged you, without saying anything, based on their previous bad experiences. This seemed quite natural and logical to Ali but it did bother him a lot and he could not take his mind off it, such that he was loosing all interest in the girl, after all he had no previous experience himself. Why should he be judged because of other people's mistakes and would be required to explain himself for another person's mischief, surely there were endless possibilities for things to go wrong.

After some time living in the West, Ali came to realise that the mere inception of the idea of having "Ali" as a boyfriend for any Western girl may bring Eastern behaviour to her mind. He was doomed from the very beginning, it didn't matter what he thought or believed, it was the culture he was carrying with him, simply due to his name. Ali found that he needed to explain certain behaviour he himself could not truly understand, despite his familiarity with the truth. It didn't even seem to be a prejudice on a Western girl's part but certain, very well justified, curiosity and possibly fear. Hence the fact that he was from the East sometimes really didn't mean much at the start of the relationship but it was always something that made him differ from the native boys. Also, it is a well known fact that Eastern men prefer or nearly always choose only "girls" to be as their wedded partner. Ali started to believe that his origins should be a problem in decision making of how to proceed with the relationship. It wasn't again really how he thought of his relationship and what he felt about the girl or he thought could become of the relationship. It was possibly only what his name suggested as to what he should be thinking of his relationship with a Western girl that seemed to matter. It didn't help that Ali didn't like to explain his feelings either, or the fact that his language difficulties did sometimes hinder him to make himself truly understood. That is even if he really wanted to reveal his feelings. So Ali concluded that he simply was being discriminated because of his place of birth and felt hurt and disappointed. Ali never wanted to be forced in his decision making for his future just to convince a girl of his good intentions. Also he didn't feel ready to make such sacrifices because he felt he still had time for marriage.

Ali knew acquaintances and friends who had married foreign girls from different countries. They were happy but somehow had lost their interest in their home country. These people he knew had concentrated on their career and only had communication with their closest family back home. Ali also knew of acquaintances and friends who had returned back home to get married. This second group obviously had tight ties back home and kept their home traditions quite well. A third group he could think of, were those who got married with a girl from their home country who they found in the West. This third group's behaviour was something in between the other two, which is best of the both world.

Ali was really wondering what was to become of him and how he could ever get out of his loneliness and find his true love. He didn't feel yet ready for marriage and thought only time will tell of what becomes of him. Ali needed to be alert for any opportunity that would come his way but meanwhile he would leave everything to his destiny.

IV

CHAPTER FOUR

Chapter 4

Epiphany, Ali's personal evolution

"Ze Daste Dideh O Del Har Do Faryad, Ke Har Che Dideh Binad Del Konad Yad. Besazom Khanjari Nishesh Ze Poolad, Zanom Bar Dideh, Ta Del Gardad Azad" (1) "One should complain of his eyes and his heart, both of them, because what is seen is hence desired. I will make a Dagger of sharp steel point, to hit to my eye's vision so as to free the heart"

Entropy always increases with time because it's the natural tendency of things to loose order. In other words, if One's life was left to its own devices, it would always tend to become less structured. Why stay in a relationship, when we live in a completely free society? Ali had come to the conclusion that his life was his own, that the gift of the Youth was a rare commodity that was given to him only once in his life and he had only one chance to use it while he was still young. Looking back on his younger years, he was regretting that he was born and lived the best years of his life in a restricted society where he had to live his life in a certain structure. However at the bottom of his heart he was unsure if living in a society with a chaotic family structure was any better. Now that he was free to live as he wished, why should he even dream of being married? He didn't know why he was thinking in this way. Maybe it was only because he had not yet met the right person in his life? Someone who complemented his personality and his short comings as a person, someone he knew he wanted and needed to add to his life in ways that he most valued. Going back to his roots, it was only now that he could understand himself and his own needs better. It was now apparent to him what kind of a spouse he most wanted because it was the first time he was listening to his heart.

Ali had finally come to an understanding to distinguish between the true love and the material world. For example an apple is a nice fruit and nothing could be truer than the saying: "an apple a day keeps the doctor away" (2). An apple is easily available everywhere and nice to have even as a decoration when fruits need to be symbolised. However, imagine you live in a famine and don't have an apple or you can't get one, then looking at one or watching a film of how it is being cut and prepared for a fruit salad would not be recommended. "Cheshme Paak" or "Clean Eye", as a word by word translation, is the best policy. You see things and will see more any time you go outside the house, because everyone likes to be attractive. Some people truly even overdo it sometimes as of how revealing their clothing can be. The solution seems to be to see but not to watch, if you happen to see something that you think is inappropriate, then you just brush your eyes past it and not look back, no matter how high the temptation. Going back to the example of the apple, it is at the moment of extreme hunger that to look at an apple or even to hold one is truly and deeply sought after by your inner desire. It is also exactly at that moment that it gets quite interesting how the people who can provide you with an apple will behave. Unfortunately if anything gets scarce, even as simple as an apple, you will begin to experience a most peculiar human behaviour. However, instead of searching for an apple, if you were to seek and find your apple tree, you should be happy. In the same way, if you dedicate your life just to find girls, then you will enter a never ending crying game. The secret to true love is to find the woman that suits you most to cherish every moment of your love with your partner and live happily ever after. Oh how fortunate are the ones who find their other half early in life. Ali was in such thoughts that he fell in a deep sleep, a long, sweet and deep sleep came over him and he felt to sink deeper and deeper into his pillow.

In his sleep Ali had a dream in which he took a selfie of himself and stared bluntly into his photo, suddenly the picture went blurry and he could see a huge image of himself as if nothing else was there. Then he started to see himself in different faces at different times of his life, his face as a boy, his face when he was a teenager and then as a young man. He could see himself also as with different characteristics such as an infant, a musician, a young physicist, a chemical student, a good mathematician, an experienced engineer, an amateur tennis player, an expert cyclist, a good swimmer and so on. Then the faces came together to form two different people, one he could recognise as himself when he left his country and another who just looked like the selfie he just had taken. Whatever he had ever seen and desired in his life came in front of his eyes whether he had managed to achieve it or not. It was only then that he could realistically see what opportunities had been open to him for his future and also the possible ways there had been to get to them. This was because he was seeing everything and at the same time. However the location of what was happening didn't seem to matter but the relevance to his future mattered. He was seeing faces that he knew were talking about him to each other, he couldn't exactly hear them but he could understand what was being said. He was even seeing things that a bit later he could connect their relevance to his future and his fate, all happening in an extremely short time, just happening in a flash. He was amazed how he knew and remembered everything, he was taking everything in. He then got really curious and looked hard to find what his future would have been if he had finally taken another route in his life. He was curious to see, for example, what would have happened if he hadn't answered that phone call and then hadn't just missed that train because of it, i.e. that he would have caught the train. He could see all the different aspects and factors that came together which lead to making a certain opportunity that he had missed. He could clearly see everything till the moment the phone rang, up until and including the time that he had answered the phone. That was when he had made the seemingly wrong decision, simply missing the train and consequently missing the opportunity. However from there on, it was blurred.

He woke up to find he had slept with lights on and he was completely drenched with sweat, he changed, switched off the lights and went back to sleep but found that he couldn't sleep. He had a look at the time but it was too early to wake up. He closed his eyes and tried to empty his mind of everything for what seemed like hours. When he finally fell asleep, he dreamt of being in prehistoric times with people not being able to speak and even covering themselves with just leaves. After several attempts, he stopped trying to speak and adopted animal like behaviour. There didn't seem to be any rules, just being good hearted and polite. If you did whatever you possibly could during the day to help out others, you were invited to a hearty meal and a place beside the fire in the evening. As a general rule, if you wanted something, you simply just pointed to it. The meaning of marriage was also unknown, men never showed any interest in anything apart from their work or better said whatever they were doing at every moment. It was women who chose men, if a woman came and pointed at you, you were the choice of her heart. Ali never saw any man ever rejecting a woman's request during the time he was there. All seemed happy and any conflicts were dealt with by the eldest in the tribe. Overall a nice cheerful society, one that made him smile when he woke up and one that always made him smile whenever he remembers his dream.

This time he woke up in the morning the next day, he felt like a new man, he felt as if most of the questions that were bothering him for so long were resolved. His dream somehow revealed to him that it is women who choose their partner and men accept the calling. A man at most could declare an interest for a woman that impresses him and can only hope for a positive outcome. Ali concluded it might be best to just suffice to choose wisely between women who show interest in him. However the most important thing was to have his partner highly respected, love her and cherish her. In other words, to have her as his "Hamsar" which means spouse but word by word means "Having the same opinion".

Ali found that the most important thing in life was to have a good heart. He couldn't help but wonder of the extent that the saying: "we make our own destiny" was true. He could clearly see two factors of it, just like the two sides of the same coin, pointing to the fact that we make our own destiny. One factor is that our true and initial intention in everything we do affects our destiny. The other factor is that we need to be fighting as hard as we can everytime to achieve our goals. So Ali tried to follow his heart, research and find out the truth about things and find out best practices that are tested in time. Then Ali would adapt a methodology and always would try to do his best to achieve his goals, no matter what obstacles he would meet in his way to achieve his wish. Ali had achieved an "awakening" because of his epiphany during his dreams and it was only in this state of awakening that Ali could hope Destiny might be on his side.

Ali changed himself to best adapt to his surroundings but kept the very best of his own culture. It's easy to get lost and waste precious time in this world, so Ali started improving his body by physical exercise and perfection of his soul by learning, thinking and contemplating in order to understand unity in life. Ali needed to become one with his surroundings, needed to unite with the world in order to make a difference.

Ali thought of the Unity or state of being one or existing as one unit as opposed to the necessity of living in pairs. In older times, people got married early and kept their love going by overseeing each others differences and faults. Their life had a structure which was mostly governed by the accepted rules of their society. For example they had their weekends to attend to each other, spend time together and relax, whether their weekend was on a Friday, Saturday, Sunday or any other day, it was irrelevant. However that structure kept them going on a successful life, which was a life where they had time to spend on things that were more important to them. They had achieved some kind of "Unity" and they were happy, children were living the love of their parents or their grandparents and were continuing their traditions. Today, we marry late and separate from the marriage early and so we spend most of our time searching for the Unity and sometimes in wrong places but most importantly we suffer while we search. We keep searching for our other half sometimes in the wrong places and so we have to keep searching indefinitely. The amount of time that we can hold on to our candles and be capable of love while being so lonely and miserable is vastly varied according to each individual but all the same, it doesn't have to be this way. That is why there is a need to revive our old traditions by understanding what was being done by our ancestors and why. It is only then that we may be able to keep our present globalisation trend and modern technology needs and prevent ourselves to go literally insane. We need to find a way to apply our ancestors traditional achievements according to today's life requirements and in order to change our each and every tradition. In other words we need to globalise our traditions from different countries and according to our contemporary requirements.

Therefore finding our other half should not be difficult. It is as if the whole Universe caters for every one of us individually and makes sure that each of us at least has the opportunity once in his life or her life to find his or her pair. When a bond is meant to happen, it's a series of everyday happenings that brings everything together. It's as if, it was meant to be, or destined to be. The whole knowledge of the world helps a man to find out how to approach his woman and being one with his surroundings. The whole knowledge of the world helps a woman to be so much full of love and affection to shock her man and attract him to be with her. Marriage needs maturity, the man and woman's relationship is a game of chaos and order which sometimes has also been referred to as the crying game. Ali was now considering marriage as an order which comes out of a chaos. Ali could see unity in every couple's life, two people who love each other and live together. Two entities working as one, helping and completing each other, sometimes even without noticing it. He could see every family as a fruit of the society which also has the potential to reproduce and give back new life to the society to keep the cycle of life, just like every fruit comes as a unit and has its seed inside. He could see every woman at the heart of the family, keeping everything together, loving and caring in order to nourish the family. Every family wife at the same time expects support from her man to achieve the family goals together.

Many things in life come as units, a grain of rice or wheat, a tree and an animal, even time comes in units of a day. A unit as a grain of wheat is a unit for which it has taken days and months to be perfected by it's plant, whether it is it's destiny to be planted back in the earth to produce more of itself or to become bread and be eaten to provide nutrition for life. So each and every grain must be respected and not wasted. Each and every constituent in a plate of food in front of us has a history before it gets ready and suitable to be eaten and should never be wasted if it could be saved for later or eaten elsewhere. Just like a single grain of wheat, every one person has a destiny in life, our goal is to pursue our destiny. Ali learnt never to underestimate himself and to try his best for his perfection. He realised, it's not what the world offers you, but it's what you can offer the world.

Ali resembled the four seasons to the total duration of human life. If we assume a life expectancy of about one hundred years, then roughly the first quarter of our lives, we are in the spring of our life. When we are half a century, 50 years old, we certainly have passed the summer of our lives. After for roughly another twenty odd years, we might find that the autumn of our life is closer than what we might think. After the third quarter, Ali would shiver at the thought that as the years pass and as we approach the winter of our life, the inevitable might happen any time. Ali was terrified at the thought that he would literally just be living in order to wait for his death.

He knew the quality of his life then, would certainly be dependent on the life he was living now. Hence with one eye to the future he tried to live a healthy life because no one knows how long he is going to live. But still the thought of living just to be waiting for his death sent chills down his spine. He considered that the only way to avoid it would be to give himself up and live for a greater cause, to dedicate his life to serve his society. He would help his society in any way possible and would stand up for his belief for a better future for everyone. In this way, death would not terminate his life, death would simply put an end to the time he is allowed to be delivering his services, an end to his entity.

V

CHAPTER FIVE

Chapter 5

Farzanehgy - Unity

"Haft shahre eshgh ra Attar gasht, ma hanouz andar khame iek koucheheim" (3)

"Attar toured seven cities of love, we are still lost in the first alley"

All his life, Ali tried his best to understand and reach the state of Farzanehgy in the path to reach Unity. Surely there was something to be done that would give him real satisfaction of being alive. Ali had realised that helping each other is what matters, he made that, the basis of his life and everything else would just spring out of this notion. For example when he went to work, he was going to a place where he was currently helping out other people and fulfilled his part in helping others to do their part for everyday life. If he was searching for a job, he was thinking of how he could best serve his society considering his personal capabilities and qualifications. Money was how he was being rewarded for what he was doing and the amount of his reward would naturally be an indication of how useful he was to the society. Ali felt happy and thankful whenever he went to the market and saw such varieties of food and services and felt the need to be moderate and wise with his shoppings. For example in a restaurant he would order only the amount of food that he would eat so in order to avoid waste and he tried his best to be exact but sensible.

"Ab ar che hameh Zolal khizad, az khordane por Malal khizad", that means: "No matter how water is crystal clear, If it be drunken too much, it will cause you harm" so he chose to be also moderate in his drinking and eating habits, even feeling slightly hungry when he stopped eating. Ali also realised that desire, hope and optimism are interconnected and so he was determined to always be positive in his life. It was an absolute necessity to wish well for others and have good intentions. In this way the universe seemed to realise your desires and turn in such ways to fulfil your wishes. However it also seemed to Ali that sometimes the whole universe seemed to oppose what you wanted to do at a specific moment and he had learnt to recognise and respect this. Of course he would not stop trying to achieve what he wants but at the same time, he realised that at such cases he needed to look back and consider all factors of his life, the effect of his actions on others and what he exactly wanted to achieve carefully. Maybe it was that the time was wrong and it wasn't yet the time for what he wanted to achieve, or that the whole concept of what he was trying to get was wrong for him or was hurting others. Possibly whatever he wanted to achieve was not ultimately good for him and so it was not destined for him to get it.

The moment he started to look in his heart for all the answers to his questions and to think deeply and logically, was the day he was re-born into his new self. He then started to see his options in life clearly and to judge right or wrong for himself. There was no question of making a mistake. Ali had realised, all that he needed to do was to look deep inside and trust in himself to find answers. He just needed to keep calm in a thunderstorm and think logically and with analytic reasoning to come to the right answer. Ali had achieved the power to find the answer in most difficult circumstances, he just knew.

He had the power of judgement and he knew where he wanted to go. For example if he needed to cook something, there was no need to re-invent the wheel and waste time trying to find out how to do it, but to refer to books or the internet for how to make the specific dish. However, there are numerous recipes for making the same dish and that's where judgement and experience comes to help. By reading the different recipes and referring to his own experience of making other dishes, he could get a feeling of what was needed to be done. The outcome is never certain but he knew he is on the right track. In this example, the goal was to cook and to find out. He needed to make his own recipe, the one that was according to his own taste. His dish should be made from ingredients that were agreeable to him and according to his own time and age. For instance, what if he would change the ghee butter to vegetable oil or change the deep frying to a simmer of the ingredients. If the outcome would still taste good, then it will certainly be a new way of cooking the same dish, a new way of doing things which is tried, tested and could later be certified for future use by everyone.

It's understood that some time after his epiphany, Ali did achieve the "Wisdom" state or "Farzanehgy", a state of unity with his environment that sprang from his clear vision of things, his better understanding of facts and all in all he felt utter love. Farzanehgy is the ultimate spiritual state a person could reach, every one of us should try to perfect oneself to reach it. Hence the path to Farzanehgy is different for each and every one of us. This path could depend on, in which country we are born, our wealth and our individual experiences in life. However although the paths are different, the true outcome is always nearly the same. So each and every individual's path to self completion is approaching Farzanehgy. All paths somehow converge to the same state of mind and behaviour all over the world which is independent of the individual's wealth or social status. Farzanehgy is a certain unified knowledge of the world and the same response to the same worldly impulses which depends only on each individual person. It's a certain sense or premonition to recognise solutions and distinguish between right or wrong and to see through situations and facts. It is a state that could be more felt and understood rather than seen and witnessed. Farzanehgy is a state of freedom from the body in order to exist but to serve the society and help each other for as long as one lives. Farzanehgy is the meaning that is hidden in every book which is comprehended after scrutinising the deeper knowledge of the book. It's the unified knowledge that makes sense across all facts that lead to the same truth. Farzanehgy is the secret of being a human and the ability to think and judge for the recognition of the best solution in every problem. The simplest, easiest, most straight forward solution to every problem, Farzanehgy is the knowledge of the world.

Ali found a job where he could serve his society and found a place where he could be useful, he started to look at everything and everyone around him differently, and he even started to see himself differently. He was not the man that had to get up to go to work, just in order to make a living. He was one person of the whole society who did a specific part that was required to make the world go around and to make tomorrow better than today for everyone. Ali started to love and respect everyone around him, he started to interpret and direct his feelings to sympathise with and help others. Ali now felt as a true part of the society and came to love the whole world around him and was watchful of how he served and became one with his surroundings.

Ali thought of the Unity or state of being one or existing as one unit as opposed to the necessity of finding a partner. In older times, people got married early and kept their love going by overseeing each others differences and faults. Their life had a structure which was mostly governed by the accepted rules of their society at the time. For example they had their weekends to attend to each other, spend time to attend to their spiritual needs and to spend time together and relax. Whether their weekend was on a Friday, a Saturday, a Sunday or any other day, it was irrelevant. However that structure kept them going on a successful life, which was a life where they had time to spend on things that were important to them. They had achieved some kind of "Unity" and they were happy, children were living the love of their parents or their grandparents and were continuing the traditions.

Unfortunately today, we marry late and separate from the marriage early and so we spend most of our time searching for Unity and sometimes in the wrong places but most importantly we suffer while we search. The amount of time that we can hold on to our candles and be capable of Love while being so lonely and miserable is vastly varied according to each individual but all the same, it doesn't have to be this way. That is why there is a need to revive our old traditions by understanding what was being done by our ancestors and why. It is only then that we maybe could keep our today's globalisation and modern technology needs and apply it, in order to change each and every tradition in different countries according to today's requirements.

It is as if the whole Universe takes care of every one of us individually and ensures that each of us at least has the opportunity once in his or her life to find his or her pair. When a bond is meant to happen, it's a series of everyday happenings that brings everything together. It's as if, it was meant to be, or destined to be. The whole knowledge of the world helps a man to find out how to approach his woman and being one with his surroundings. The whole knowledge of the world helps a woman to be so much full of love and affection to shock her man and lure him to be with her. Marriage needs maturity, the man-woman relationship is a game of chaos and order which sometimes has also been referred to as the crying game. Ali was now considering marriage as an order which comes out of a chaos. Ali could see unity in every couple's life, two persons who love each other and live together. Two entities working as one, helping and completing each other, sometimes even without noticing it. He could see every family as a fruit of the society which also has the potential to reproduce and give back new life to the society to keep the cycle of life, just like every fruit comes as a unit and has its seed inside. He could see every woman at the heart of the family, keeping everything together, loving and caring in order to nourish the family. Every family wife at the same time expects support from her man to achieve the family goals together.

Even here in the West, it used to be: "I give you my hand, my heart, and my love, from this day forward and for as long as we both shall live". The problem with our day and age is that today, we break bonds easily and the concept of living happily ever after has lost its meaning for most of us. Is it not our today's way of life hindering us from seeing our true opportunities and hence our destiny in life? Could it be that if we chose a more solemn, more reserved attitude to life, if we were more concentrated to a most wanted goal and chose to be patience for it, then maybe life would also reward us, then we should be more likely to see the opportunities in life and grab them. If we could try to understand Farzanehgy and feel Unity, maybe we could be better citizens of Earth and the world would be a better place.

We forget that we are here to perfect ourselves, if we have children, the same perfection continues to our children, simply because we can never be perfect. However we can teach what we have learnt to our children. As our children have at least partially our genes, they are prone to the same mistakes that we have made in our lives. Teaching our experiences to our children should be a continuous endeavour, a search for the right moment to explain what we have in mind to convey to them. Sometimes children are quick to grasp what is being explained and don't seem to have the same difficulties as yourself to understand the subject but sometimes they don't seem to be able to grasp what you want to tell them. It needs patience, persistence and perseverance in order to give the right message to them and in full and it takes a long time. So the earlier we spend time with our children the better because we have more time to convey our information to our beloved ones. Children are like a fruit and when it ripens, it gets separated from the tree, sooner or later they will leave you, so the more time spent between family may lead to higher ingredients that they could be taken off you. "Anche Javan dar Ayeneh binad, Pir An dar kheshteh kham mibinad" or "what a young person sees in the mirror, an old person sees it in unbaked bricks" so as grown-ups it's also our responsibility to give guidance to our children for the future and according to our own experience but always considering the change of time and according to the contemporary standards of living.

Ali found his lifetime love, he was no longer alone but living with his partner. It didn't matter how he met with his lifetime love or even where he met her. It was only important that he had found her. The moment he saw her, he knew she was the one, he liked everything about her at first sight, even the way she moved or talked. It had been long time now that Ali felt he needed to end his futile solo life and he thought why not now, why not with her. Ali shared his true intentions to her and their first kiss and then their marriage was only a few days away.

It was not a simple process by any means, but Ali finally had started thinking as "we" and not "I" and that's how he realised his true love. Internally the two faces of himself as he had once seen in his dream, now were not there any more, they were burning away in the flames of his love to give shape to his new self. The fire inside of him was unbearable, the desire to be with his other half and to provide for her. Ali felt his old self melting away, seeking to fill the gaps existing in his partner. Ali found true love can only exist, when he managed to put an end to his self and evolve as supplement to his other half. Ali felt unity in his new life only to realise that the state of unity was never static but evolved all the time because it was dependent also on his partner. His partner, their lives and he himself were changing all the time. Their love was exactly the same act of the crying game, but now looked at in a different way. It was just like love and hate that could be considered as the two sides of the same coin. The result was now a fruit that belonged to the two of them, a loving being that shared their bodily characteristics and was their mirror when they looked deep in their baby's eyes.

Ali considered Love to be like a candle, a candle inside each and every one of us. However, this candle is not for ever because we die one day. It's only the "Einheit" or the "Unity" candle which is burning for ever but we are all mortals and in order to keep the candle running, we need each other. It's amazing how beautiful is the feeling of unity while it lasts and how sweet the fruit of Love is when it comes. It ripens for nine months and changes life forever. It comes as a blessing, a completion of love, a fruit of Unity to keep the couple's candle lit for ever.

Ali now had seen the light beyond the seven cities of love or the seven phases of Chakra, no matter how anyone wanted to name it. He felt that he had achieved the state of Unity or Farzanehgy. Ali had realised that the state of unity or Farzanehgy is the same, it was the result, no matter if the route to this state was different for every single one of us. As the result was the same, no matter whatever route taken to achieve the state, so the unity itself had different shapes. It took shapes in accordance to the individual, ones place of living, his or her status of life or even at what age he or she achieved his or her state of unity or Farzanehgy. Ali realised that Farzanehgy evolves and changes all the time according to the conditions of life, the societies requirements or simply in changes in ones surroundings.

Ali had grasped the true meaning of life.

GLOSSARY

Glossary

Ab ar che hameh Zolal khizad, az khordane por Malal khizad: No matter how water is crystal clear, If it be drunken too much, it will cause you harm, Persian saying.

Bazaar: Bazaar is a market.

Chador: Chador is kind of a Hejab, it's a long cloth used to cover the whole body except for the face, wrapped around loosely and held tightly with one hand below the chin.

Destiny: "Destiny", "Sarnevesht" or "Tagdir "could be explained as almost a magical outcome to an event, or equally successive occurrence of certain unexpected events that eventually would shape the future of a person.

Einheit: German Einheit is "Unity" in English as word for word translation but it's the condition of being One or existing as one which is referred in here.

Eye: "Eye" could be explained as almost a magical interaction of people between themselves where the extreme desire of a person towards other people's looks or possession, could eventually have a negative affect on them.

Gheirat: Gheirat is the zest with which everyone would be fighting with the slightest mention of the smallest unsuitable comment or gesture against their Holy, this zest is called Gheirat.

Hamsar: "Hamsar" which means spouse but word by word means "Having the same mind".

Haya: Haya is the refusal of a person to provoke, for example for a girl by wearing Hejb.

Hejab: Hejab is any kind of a covering used in order to hide different part of one's body out of sight, for example Chador or Rousari, a veil.

Ieki boud, ieki naboud, gheir az Khoda hich kas naboud: This is usual way of beginning to tell a story in the East and basically means Once upon a time.

Mahram: Mahram is the condition of allowed intimacy and it's granted by birth such as for example the intimacy between a mother and his son. However the same word is also used to describe the intimacy between husband and wife as granted by marriage.

Mehrieh: Mehrieh or dowry is the amount of money the groom promises as insurance for the bride to guarantee her future should the marriage be broken up.

Namous: One's mother, sister and later on one's wife and even one's country were considered to be one's Namous and needed to be defended from blasphemy and attack at all cost.

Taqas: Taqas could be explained as the unexplained influence of your actions on your fate, it is roughly translated in English as Karma

Tavoun: Tavoun is an amount of money or anything else, given to you in replacement for something broken or lost.

Vozou: Vozou is a cleaning procedure necessary to be done prior to praying and is done by mainly cleaning face, hands and feet briefly with water.

REFERENCES

References

1. "Ze Daste Dideh O Del Har Do Faryad, Ke Har Che Dideh Binad Del Konad Yad. Besazom Khanjari Nishesh Ze Poolad, Zanom Bar Dideh, Ta Del Gardad Azad" Persian saying from Baba Taher Oryan Hamadani, Googled July 2020
2. "An apple a day keeps the doctor away", Well-known statement based on an 1860s Welsh proverb, Googled 11/09/2021
3. Farid ud-Din Attar of Nishapur, A Persian poet and Theoretician of Sufism